SOMETHING SPECIAL FOR ME

by Vera B. Williams

Greenwillow Books

An Imprint of HarperCollinsPublishers

Something Special for Me
Copyright © 1983 by Vera B. Williams
All rights reserved.
Manufactured in China by South China Printing Company Ltd.
For information address HarperCollins Children's Books,
a division of HarperCollins Publishers,
10 East 53rd Street, New York, NY 10022.
www.harperchildrens.com

With special thanks to Savannah

Library of Congress Cataloging-in-Publication Data

Williams, Vera B.
Something special for me.
"Greenwillow Books."
Summary: Rosa has difficulty choosing a special birthday present
to buy with the coins her mother and grandmother have saved,
until she hears a man playing beautiful music on an accordion.
[1. Family life—Fiction. 2. Gifts—Fiction. 3. Music—Fiction.] I. Title.
PZ7.W6685So 1983 [E] 82-11884
ISBN 0-688-01806-8 (trade)
ISBN 0-688-01807-6 (lib. bdg.)
ISBN 0-688-06526-0 (pbk.)

10 11 12 13 SCP 20 19 First Edition

Our new chair has cocoa on one arm now. It isn't brand-new anymore, but Grandma and Mama and I still like to squeeze into it together just like the day we first brought it home. That was when Aunt Ida, who lives upstairs, took this picture of us. We keep it on the shelf next to the big money jar and the picture of me when I was one month old.

One Saturday Mama and I were sitting in the chair in our bathrobes. I kept trying to talk to Mama about my birthday which was going to be in just three days, but Mama wouldn't listen. On her day off from her job at the Blue Tile Diner, Mama loves to sit and read her newspaper. Then she never even hears the things I tell her. I had to tickle her foot until she threw down the paper and jumped out of the chair.

Then she chased me all over the house.

When she caught me, she held me up to the mirror. "Who's that kid who won't let her own mother enjoy her well-earned rest even on Saturday?" she said, making her mad face. I made my monster face. We made faces in the mirror till we laughed so much we had to pee. Then Mama hugged me tight. "You're much more fun than any newspaper," she said.

Then we studied the money in the big jar. The jar is only partly full now. But one time Grandma and Mama and I saved up so much money that jar was full to the top. That was when we went shopping and bought a chair for my mother. There was some money left even after we paid for the chair. Now we still put money in the jar every Friday when Mama brings her tips home from work. If I help out at the diner, I put money in the jar too, and Grandma puts in whatever she can spare.

"What are we going to spend the money on this time?" I asked Mama.

She lifted down the jar and dumped it and me right into the chair. She called my grandma over too. "Mother," she said, "it's going to be Rosa's birthday in three days. The chair was really for you and me. Don't you think it's Rosa's turn to get something special?"

Grandma thought it was a wonderful idea. "Why don't you take

Rosa downtown shopping? Whatever you buy will be from me too."

"And it will be from Aunt Ida and Uncle Sandy too. Whenever they get their pay they drop money in our jar," I said.

Mama and I got dressed fast and Grandma changed the money into dollar bills. As we went out the door, she hollered after us, "Rosa, you buy something real nice."

I knew just what would be real nice, so we went right to the skate store. I tried on skates. I skated up and down in the store. My friends Leora and Jenny and Mae all have new skates, and I really wanted them too.

I could see myself dancing around on my new skates in the schoolyard to Leora's little radio. Then, just as the man was about to wrap up the box and Mama and I were about to pay for the skates, I wasn't so sure I wanted them.

I wanted them, but I could tell that skates weren't really what I wanted to empty that big jar of money for. Not even white skates with orange wheels that could race and dance all over the street.

So we went out of the store without buying anything.

Across the street was the department store, and I pulled Mama through the revolving door and up the escalator to the children's floor. There I tried on dresses and I tried on coats. I tried on shoes and even hats. I looked at myself all around in the big mirrors.

I imagined standing just like that with Leora and Jenny and Mae outside the variety store on my birthday. "I want these," I said to Mama, "the polka dot dress with its own jacket and the blue shoes with crisscross straps and little heels."

Then just as they were about to wrap them up and Mama and I were about to pay for them, I wasn't sure I really wanted them so much. I wanted them, but I could tell that new shoes and a new dress, even with its own jacket, were not the special presents I wanted to empty the big jar for. So we went out of the department store without buying anything.

Then right down the block I saw a red tent in the store window. Next to it was a blue sleeping bag and a knapsack with pockets all over it. The sleeping bag was spread out all ready for the night. I pushed open the door and Mama followed me into that store.

I could just see how it would be to go on a trip in Aunt Ida and Uncle Sandy's truck. Leora and Jenny and Mae would come along. I'd pack everything we needed into the knapsack. Then we'd put up the tent by the lake and we'd all sleep in it together: This is what I *really* want, I told my mother.

But when the salesperson was wrapping it all up and Mama and I were about to pay for it, I got that feeling again. This was not the exact present I wanted to empty that whole jar for. Mama recognized the look on my face. And when we walked out of that store without any packages, Mama was laughing.

But I started to cry. "What if I can't ever decide? What if I end up with no birthday present at all, what if even my next birthday comes and I still can't decide?"

Mama wiped my tears. "Don't worry," she said. "You have a few days yet till your birthday. Let's stop in the Blue Tile Diner and have a treat while you think about it some more."

Josephine, who is the owner, brought us our pie
and ice cream herself. She played my favorite songs on the
jukebox too. "For an early birthday," she said. "Many happy
returns of the day." After that I felt better. I was ready to look in
more stores. But it had gotten too late. We could already see a
star in the sky.

"Quick, Rosa, make a wish," my mama said.

"Star light, star bright

First star I see tonight

I wish I may, I wish I might

Have the wish I wish tonight,"

I whispered. But all that I could wish was that I would know
what to wish for.

And right after that is when I heard the music.

We were standing near the corner, and someone was standing under the lamppost playing on an instrument.

"What is that?" I asked my mother.

"An accordion," she told me. "Your other grandma used to play one just like that. She played at concerts in the park and at weddings. I remember people used to say she could make even the chairs and tables dance."

On the way home I imagined myself playing the accordion while the chairs and tables danced. I could see Leora and Jenny and Mae dancing too. I could see myself right up on the stage in the park.

I imagined myself sitting on our back steps and playing music whenever I wanted.

On my birthday, Grandma and Aunt Ida and Uncle Sandy and I took the money and went to meet Mama at the music store. The music store was full of big accordions, but they were very expensive. Then the woman in the store said, "How about this one? It's good for a beginner." And she showed me one just the right size for me. When she played it, I heard the same beautiful sounds I had heard on the corner by the diner.

We were lucky because that accordion wasn't brand-new, so it cost less than the others.

It took all the jar money though and a little bit more from Aunt Ida's purse. Uncle Sandy said he'd pay for lessons every week. And this time I didn't want to change my mind at all.

Next morning I was sure I had chosen exactly right. Through the door I could see our chair. I could see our big jar with just one dime in it for good luck. Grandma and Mama were making breakfast in the kitchen.

And right beside my bed was my own accordion
waiting for me to make songs come out of it.